THIS BOOK BELONGS TO:

Adam Jackson

meomi

WOULD LIKE TO DEDICATE THIS BOOK TO
SECRET SQUIRREL STASHES, MUNKI TEACUP PARTIES,
OUR FAMILY & FRIENDS

MEOMI is the creative team of Vicki Wong and Michael C. Murphy who live in Vancouver, Canada with their many sasquatch friends. They enjoy writing silly stories, drinking tea, and drawing strange creatures. Meomi's art and animation has been featured in books, toys and projects worldwide. Visit them at: www.meomi.com

CHECK OUT THE OTHER BOOKS TOO - I HEAR THEY'RE PRETTY GOOD! GRUMBLE!

First published in hardback in the USA by Immedium Inc. in 2007
First published in hardback and paperback in Great Britain by HarperCollins Children's Books in 2009

10 9 8 7 6 5

ISBN: 978-0-00-731252-8

HarperCollins Children's Books is a division of HarperCollins Publishers Ltd.

Text and illustrations copyright © MEOMI Design Inc.: Vicki Wong and Michael Murphy 2007

Published by arrangement with Immedium Inc. immedium www.immedium.com

Visit our website at www.harpercollins.co.uk
Printed in Italy

Edited by Don Menn
Design by Meomi and Stefanie Liang

Please be kind to shadows.

THE OCTONAUTS

& the Sea of Shade

· MEOMI ·

HarperCollins *Children's Books*

It was a quiet afternoon under the deep green sea when...

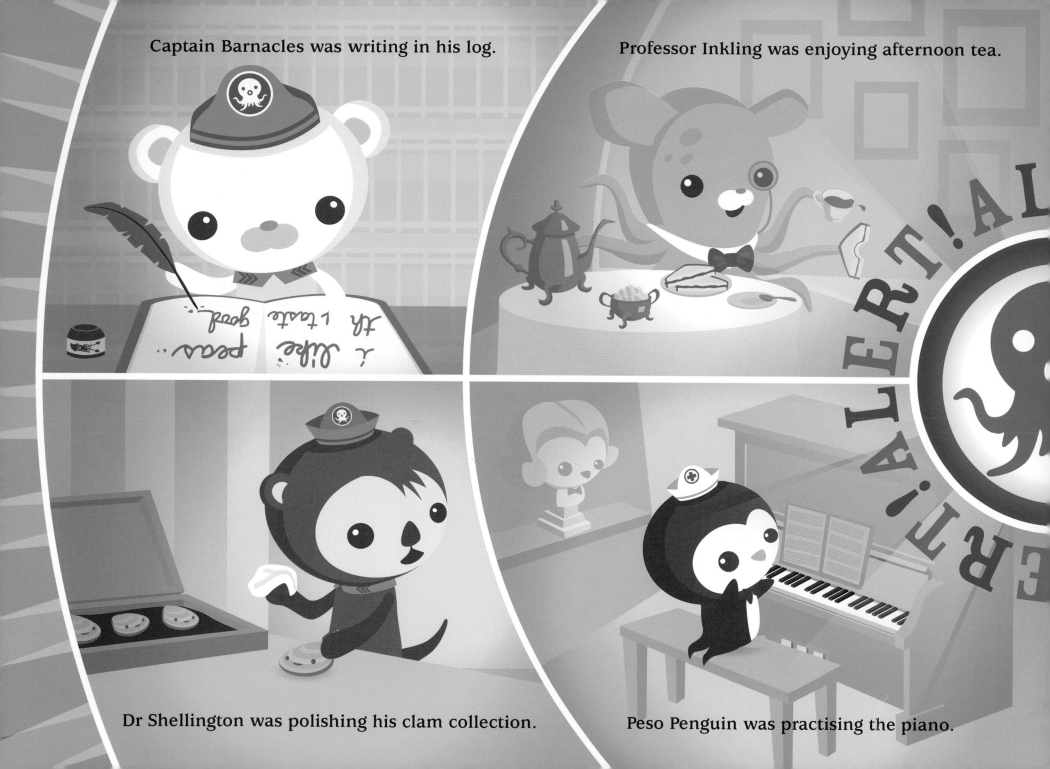

Captain Barnacles was writing in his log.

Professor Inkling was enjoying afternoon tea.

Dr Shellington was polishing his clam collection.

Peso Penguin was practising the piano.

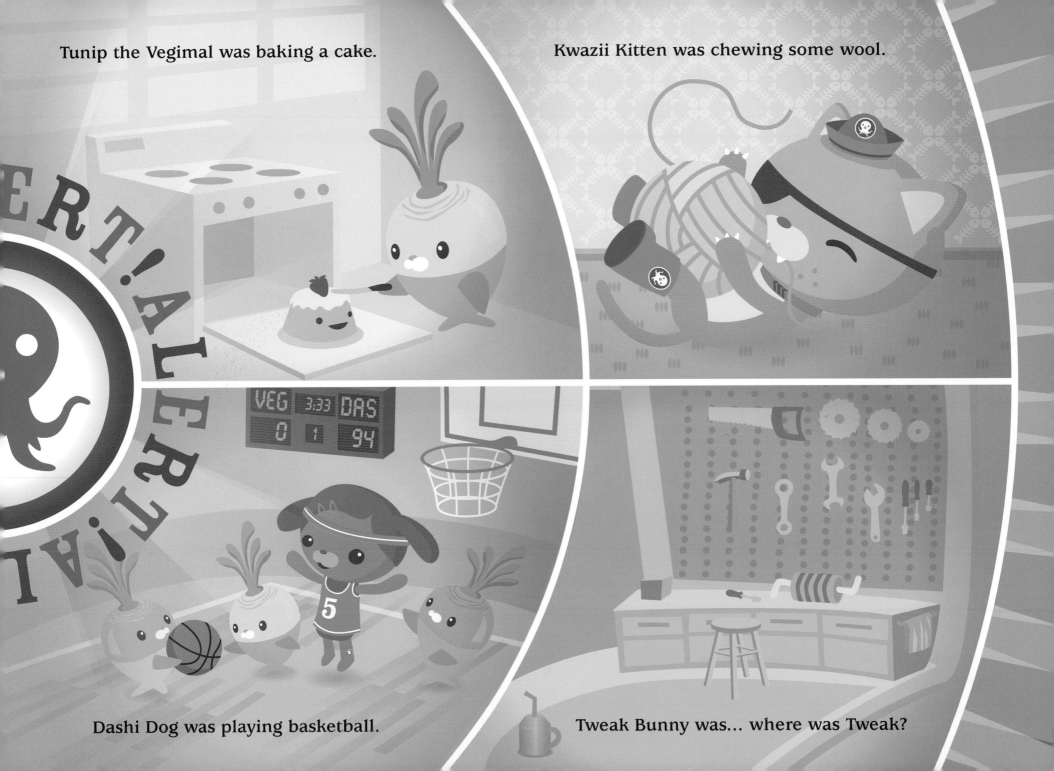

Tunip the Vegimal was baking a cake.

Kwazii Kitten was chewing some wool.

Dashi Dog was playing basketball.

Tweak Bunny was... where was Tweak?

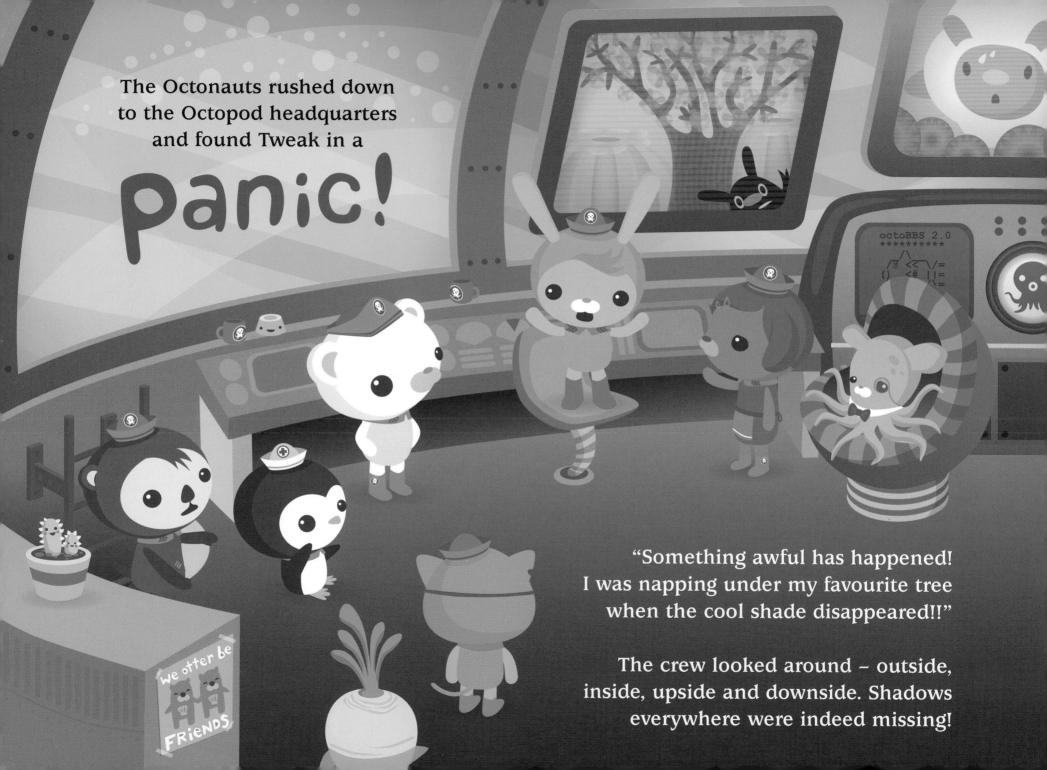

The Octonauts rushed down to the Octopod headquarters and found Tweak in a

Panic!

octoBBS 2.0

we otter be FRiENDS

"Something awful has happened! I was napping under my favourite tree when the cool shade disappeared!!"

The crew looked around – outside, inside, upside and downside. Shadows everywhere were indeed missing!

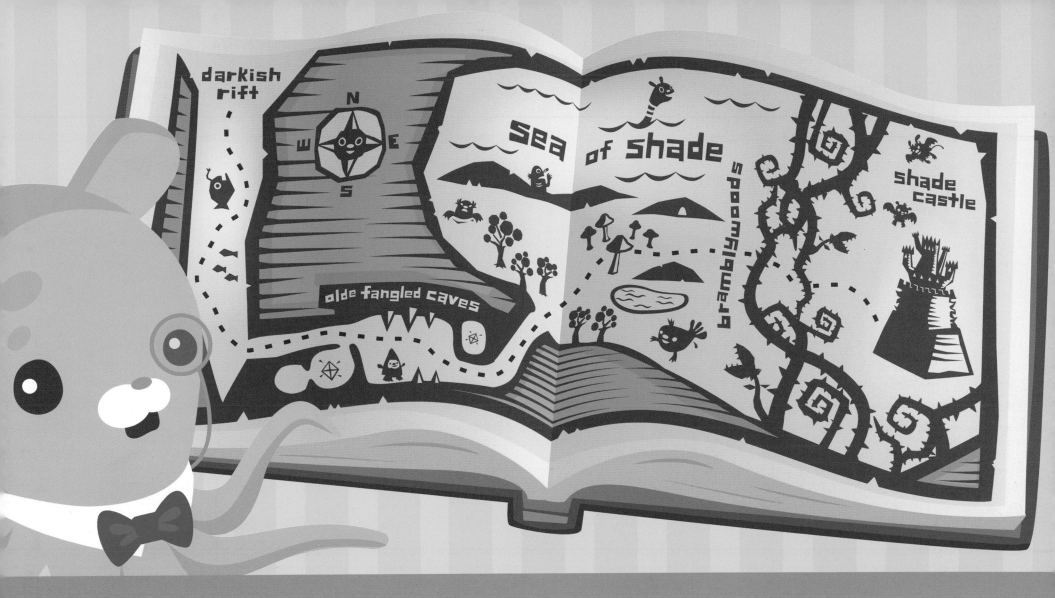

"Something must be wrong in the Sea of Shade!"
Professor Inkling exclaimed, as he carefully selected a large book from the shelf.
"According to the *Mysterious Places Guide*, this hidden realm is ruled by
a great Shade King who governs the shadows of the world.
Octonauts, you must talk to the King and discover what is causing this disturbance!"

"But how will we find him?"
Kwazii Kitten meowed gruffly.

"Hmm... a very interesting question!"
Professor Inkling muttered.

"Using cartographic bathymetry
to calculate the compasserific
co-ordinates contained on this
superannuated substrate should
yield the location!"

The befuddled Octonauts stared
at Professor Inkling.

"Errr... follow this old map!"

PREPARE to LAUNCH!

Dashi called over the speakers.

The Octonauts packed their supplies
for the long journey ahead. Tunip made
the crew a fresh batch of barnacle
biscuits to eat along the way.

They cautiously dived down the ocean's darkest rift, waving to friendly fronds and slipping past sleeping sharks, until they reached the entrance to the Olde Fangled Caves.

Inside the caverns, the Octonauts were confused for days.
Which side was up and which side was down?

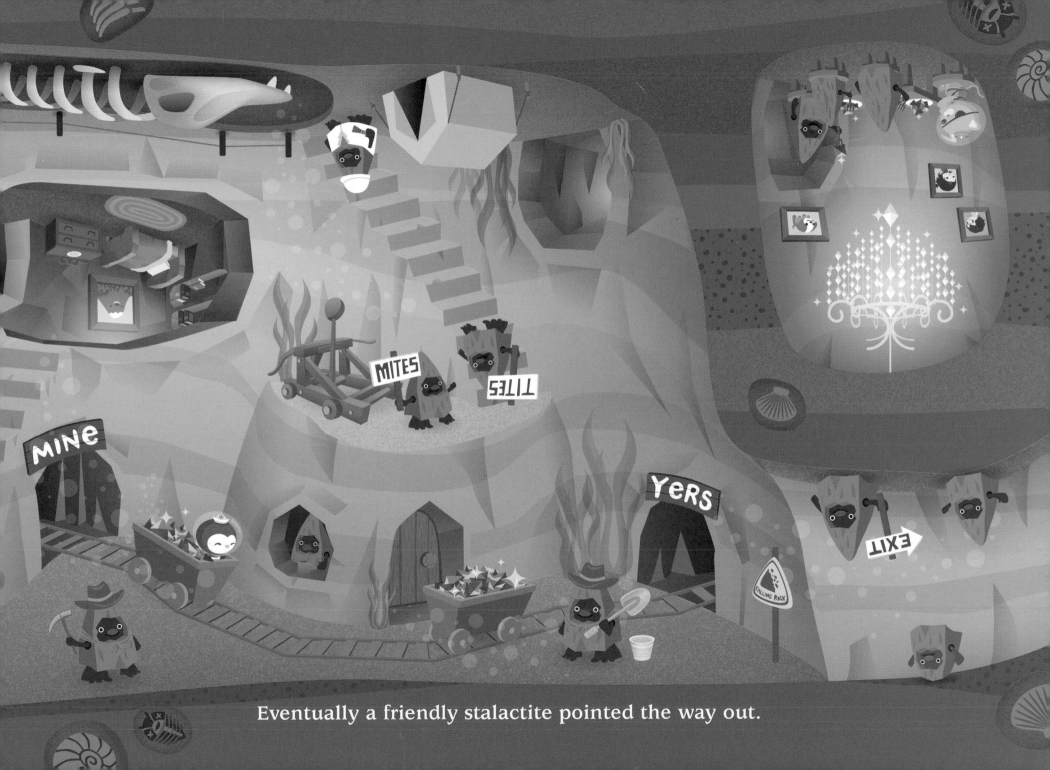

Eventually a friendly stalactite pointed the way out.

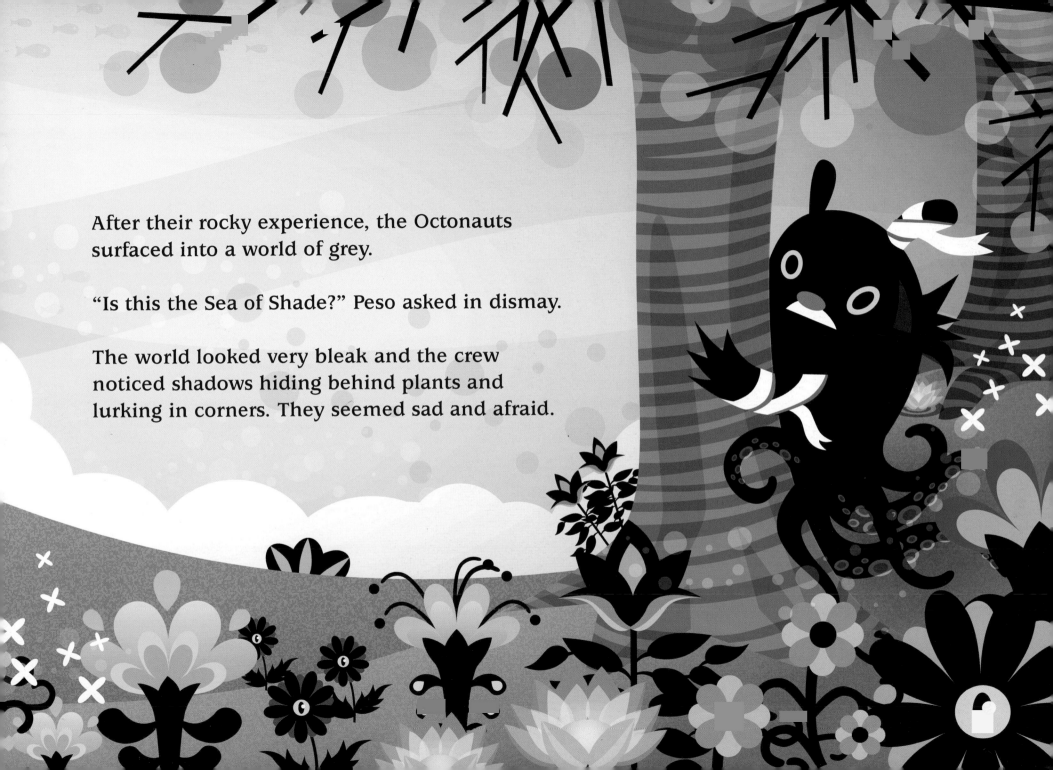

After their rocky experience, the Octonauts surfaced into a world of grey.

"Is this the Sea of Shade?" Peso asked in dismay.

The world looked very bleak and the crew noticed shadows hiding behind plants and lurking in corners. They seemed sad and afraid.

"This place needs some cheering up!"
Barnacles declared, as he pulled out his
accordion and began playing a happy shanty.

In the warm glow of the ship's beams,
flowers blossomed and the leaves turned
wonderful colours. Curious shadows slowly
came out to watch.

The lights and music reminded the shades of the outside world where there were lots of things to see and do.

They happily followed the Octonauts, as they travelled deeper into the sea.

Finally, the Octonauts came upon
a vast thicket of black, thorny branches
that twined and tangled in all directions.

"The Shade King lives on the other
side of these Bramblywoods, but there's
no way our ship can pass through... and the
monsters up top don't look friendly,"
Tweak glumly concluded.

Wanting to help, the shadows pooled their shady thoughts.
They could merge together and form a ship to carry the Octonauts!

"Only shadows could pass through a shadow forest,"
Barnacles remarked in appreciation. The Octonauts quickly boarded
and to everyone's relief, they slipped into the thicket with ease.

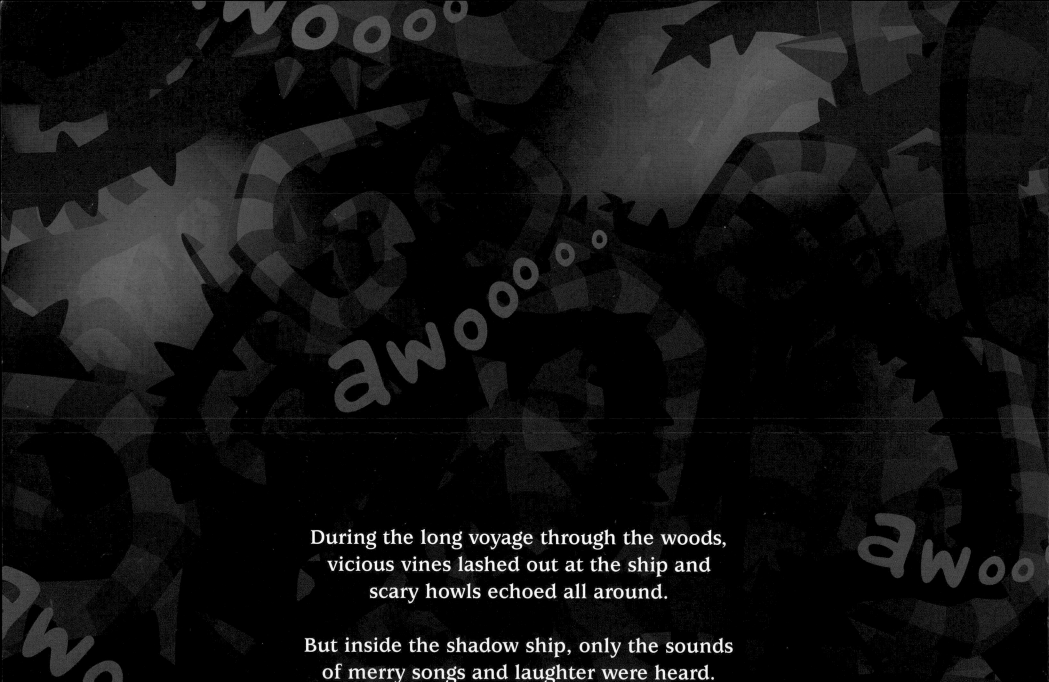

During the long voyage through the woods,
vicious vines lashed out at the ship and
scary howls echoed all around.

But inside the shadow ship, only the sounds
of merry songs and laughter were heard.

When the crew reached the end of Bramblywoods, they could see the sinister Shade Castle looming in the distance with a large palace guard waiting at the gate.

The Shade King greatly disliked being disturbed by strangers and
scowled as the Octonauts were escorted into the Great Hall.
Captain Barnacles removed his hat and gave a deep bow.
"Your Majesty, we miss our shadows very much... why did they leave?"

The King frowned. "For centuries, I watched through my Shade-o-scope as shadows were stepped on and ignored. It's not easy to follow someone around all day, but we never get any thanks. Some people are even afraid of their own shadows!

Everyone would be happier if we just lived in our own worlds. That is why I called all my subjects home to the Sea of Shade."

"Please look again," Peso pleaded. "Everyone is so sad without any shade. We've learned how important shadows are. Please let them come back, Your Highness!"

The Shade King grudgingly peered into his Shade-o-scope and was surprised by what he saw.

He turned back to his court only to see glum faces looking up at him. The shades missed their friends on the outside, too.

"Very well. You may all return..." the King decided, "*IF* the Octonauts agree to be our Shade Ambassadors and help remind everyone to appreciate their shadows!"

"Thank you, Your Majesty!" Barnacles accepted their new position with pride.

We'll do our best!

"Go, my shady subjects!" the King
proclaimed. "Return to your friends!"

That night everyone enjoyed a big party to celebrate
the first-ever Shadow Appreciation Day!

THE end

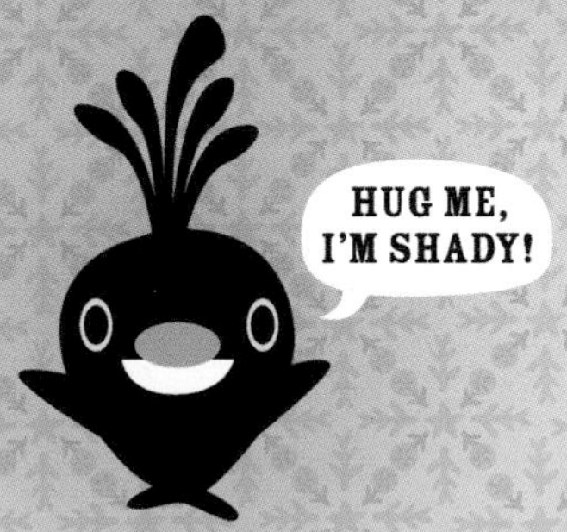

MEET THE OCTONAUTS!

CAPTAIN BARNACLES BEAR

Brave Captain Barnacles is a polar bear extraordinaire and the leader of the Octonauts crew. He's always the first to rush in and help whenever there's a problem. Besides adventuring, Barnacles enjoys playing his accordion and writing in his captain's log.

KWAZII KITTEN

Kwazii is a daredevil orange kitten with a mysterious pirate past. He loves excitement and travelling to exotic places. His favourite hobbies include long baths, racing the GUP-B, and general swashbuckling.

PESO PENGUIN

Peso is the medic for the team. He enjoys putting bandages on cuts and tending to wounds. He's not fond of scary things, but if a creature is hurt or in danger, he can be the bravest Octonaut of all!

SHELLINGTON SEA OTTER

Dr Shellington is a nerdy sea otter scientist who loves doing field research and working in his lab. He's easily distracted by rare plants and animals, which sometimes gets him into trouble. His knowledge of the ocean and its creatures is a big help in Octonaut missions.

TWEAK BUNNY

Tweak is the engineer for the Octopod. She keeps everything working properly in the launch bay and maintains the Octonauts' subs: GUP-A to GUP-E. Tweak likes all kinds of machinery and enjoys tinkering with strange contraptions that sometimes work in unexpected ways.

DASHI DOG

Dashi is a sweet dachshund who oversees operations in the Octopod HQ and launch bay. She monitors the computers and manages all ship traffic. She's also the Octonauts' official photographer and enjoys taking photos of undersea life.

PROFESSOR INKLING OCTOPUS

Professor Inkling is a brilliant Dumbo octopus oceanographer. He founded the Octonauts with the intention of furthering underwater research and preservation. Because of his delicate, big brain, he prefers to help the team from his library in the Octopod.

TUNIP THE VEGIMAL

Tunip is one of many Vegimals, a special underwater critter (part vegetable / part animal) who help out around the Octopod. They speak their own language that only Shellington can understand (sometimes!). Vegimals love to cook and bake: kelp cakes, kelp cookies, kelp soufflé...